BOOK 4
Big Stink

MAC PARK

Illustrated by JAMES HART

ALLEN&UNWIN
SYDNEY · MELBOURNE · AUCKLAND · LONDON

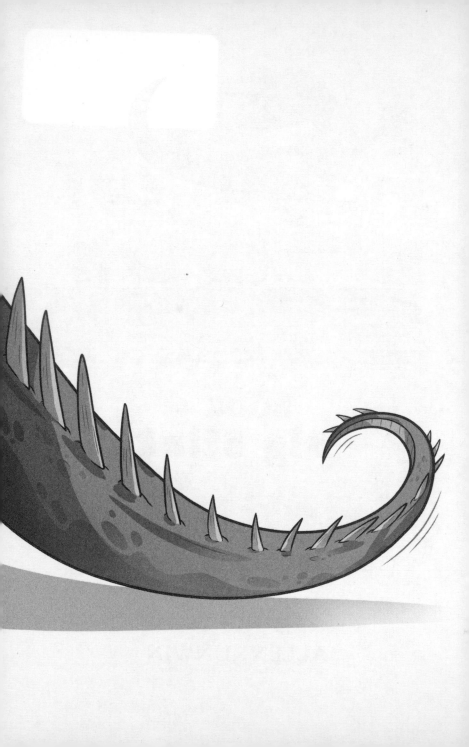

Chapter One

Hunter Marks was lying on the ground. He was in a forest clearing, near a waterfall. He wanted to get to his d-bot, but he was too weak.

I'm going to fail at being a D-Bot Squad member, Hunter thought sadly. *All because of a giant stinky fart.*

A stegosaurus had done the biggest fart Hunter had ever heard. The giant cloud of toxic gas had made Hunter so dizzy he'd passed out.

Hunter tried to lift his head. When he did, he saw the steg looking at him.

Charlie told me to wait for her, he thought. *Why didn't I listen?*

The steg farted once more.

Flrrrrrpt! Braaaaapt!

Then Hunter's world spun and everything went black again.

Hunter and Charlie were meant
to catch the steg together. But
Hunter had been ready first.

He'd teleported to the forest
alone. He hadn't told anyone
that he was leaving. Not
Charlie. Not even Ms Stegg,
the head of Dino Corp.

'Charlie to Hunter, can you hear me?' Charlie's voice boomed from the d-band on Hunter's wrist.

But Hunter was not awake.

Charlie tried again.

'Hunter? It's Charlie. I'm here, in the forest. I'm coming to you now. I hope you're okay.'

Meanwhile, the steg began to move.

Thud! Thud! Thud! Thud!

The steg stomped around the clearing in a wide circle. Farts flew from its bottom.

Thud! Thud! **Thud!** **Thud!**

Flrrrrrpt! Braaaaapt! Phrrrrrr!

Thud! Flrrrrrpt!
Thud! Braaaaapt!
Thud! Thud! Phrrrrrr!

The ground shook with every step it took.

The shaking ground woke
Hunter. He opened his eyes and
saw the steg heading for him.

Not more toxic gas! Hunter
thought.

He tried to move, but he
couldn't. His head pounded.

I need to get out of here, Hunter thought. *It might stomp on me. But I'm so dizzy.*

Bang! Crash!

'Oh no,' Hunter mumbled. The steg had knocked over his d-bot.

Flrrrrrpt! Braaaaapt! Phrrrrrr!

Hunter tried holding his breath. *The less of this toxic air I breathe, the better,* he thought. *I really need to move! But how?*

And then...

Crunch!

'**No!**' Hunter yelled. The steg weighed 3000 kilos – as much as an elephant. And it had just squashed his d-bot!

Hunter rolled onto his tummy.

I'll crawl away! he thought.

'Groooowl!'

The steg was getting so close now.

*Now, Hunter. Hurry. Come on,
you can do this*, he thought.

But the steg farted once more.
It was the worst one yet.

Flrrrrrppppppttttt!
Phrrrrrrrrrrr!

Hunter's head spun wildly. His eyes stung. His nose and lungs burned. Just as everything went black again, he heard the biggest noise yet.

'Rooaar!'

Chapter Two

Charlie also heard the steg's roar. She knew she was getting close. She climbed down from her d-bot and left it hidden in the ferns.

Charlie crept towards the noise.
'Uurgh,' she whispered. 'It smells
horrible here. It must be steg
farts. I'd better use my gas
mask.'

Charlie pushed a button on the
side of her helmet. Instantly,
her face was covered with a
mask.

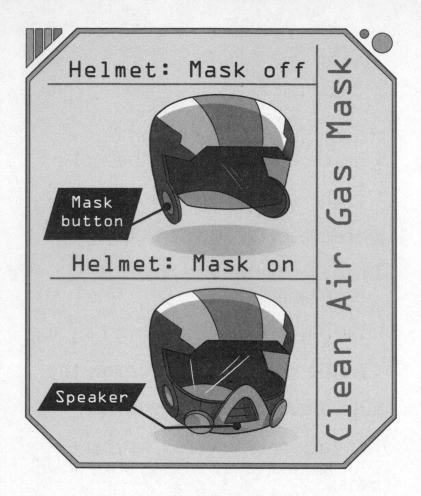

Helmet: Mask off

Mask button

Helmet: Mask on

Speaker

Clean Air Gas Mask

'No more stinky, toxic air for me,' she said. 'D-Bot Squad sure has thought of everything!'

Then all Charlie could hear was farting.

Flrrrrrpt! Braaaaapt! Phrrrrrr!

She giggled. 'You really are just one big walking fart, aren't you, steggie? Just like all the books I've read said you were.'

The stegosaurus was one of Charlie's favourite dinosaurs.

Charlie spotted Hunter near the waterfall and gasped.

'He isn't wearing his gas mask. He left before Ms Stegg could tell him about it. No wonder he's passed out!' Charlie cried.

Then she saw Hunter's d-bot. 'The steg must have walked right over the top of it!'

Thud! Flrrrrrpt! Thud Braaaaapt!

The steg was getting ready to stomp on Hunter.

'No!' Charlie shouted. She took a small packet from her tool belt. Then she raced towards the steg.

'Hey,' yelled Charlie. 'Over here,
you big old dinosaur. Come
and get your yummy lunch.'

Charlie added some water from
her water bottle to the packet.
It grew. She tipped it and moss
came out. It grew even more as
it hit the ground.

'Look! Now I have a huge pile
of food for you.'

The dinosaur turned and sniffed.

'Yes, come and get it,' Charlie called.

Flrrrrrpt! Braaaaapt! Phrrrrrr!

'Uuuuurgh! You are amazing and disgusting all at once!' Charlie yelled.

Thud! Thud! Braaaaapt!

Thud! Thud! Phrrrrrrrrrrr!

Charlie felt the ground shake
with every step the steg took.

'That's right, steggie,' she shouted.
'Good dino, come to me.'

Slowly the dinosaur moved
towards Charlie. And away
from Hunter.

Charlie let out a breath.
'You're far enough away from
Hunter now,' she said. 'Here's
your lunch!'

As the dinosaur started eating
the moss, Charlie ran over to
Hunter.

'Hunter!' she cried. 'Wake up!'

Charlie took her water bottle
from her belt. She opened the
lid and splashed water in
Hunter's face.

'Aaargh,' Hunter groaned.
'I'm so dizzy and sleepy.'

'You need your gas mask,' Charlie said. She hit the button on his helmet.

The mask came down over Hunter's face. All at once he could breathe again.

'Clean air!' he cheered. 'Air that doesn't sting, burn and stink! Those dino-farts are deadly!'

'Totally!' said Charlie. 'Do you think you can get up now?'

'I hope so,' Hunter said, sitting up. 'I didn't know our helmets had gas masks. We can talk through them, too!'

'Yep, Ms Stegg told me about them back at base,' Charlie said. 'You'd already left.'

'Oh,' said Hunter as he got up slowly. He looked at Charlie, then looked away. *Here it comes,* he thought. *She's cross with me for not doing what I was told.*

Hunter took a deep breath. 'I know I should have waited...' he began.

'Hunter, it's okay,' Charlie said.

'No, I should have waited for you,' Hunter said. 'I'm…um… I just—'

'You wanted to get to the dinosaur. You're happy working alone. I get it. I really do.'

Hunter blinked. 'You like working on your own too?' he asked.

'Yeah,' Charlie said. 'Sometimes. But at D-Bot Squad, being a team can be a good thing, too.'

Hunter pushed at the dirt with his foot. 'Do you think you could help me fix my d-bot?'

'No problem!' said Charlie.

Chapter Three

Charlie took a tool from her tool belt. 'This will pop those panels back into shape. It sucks the dents out.' She handed the tool to Hunter.

'Thanks, that's just what I need,' Hunter said. 'Thank goodness the steg has forgotten us.' He started working on his d-bot.

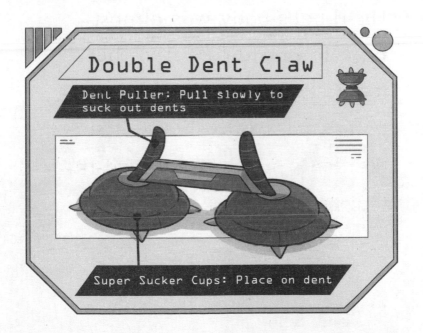

Double Dent Claw

Dent Puller: Pull slowly to suck out dents

Super Sucker Cups: Place on dent

'The steg's happy eating over there for now,' agreed Charlie.

'Nice work with the moss,' said Hunter. He pulled the double dent claw's handles. **Pop! Pop!** His d-bot's body was almost back to normal.

'Those moving rods around your d-bot's head were a good idea, too,' Charlie said.

'They helped me through the thick forest,' Hunter agreed. 'What changes did you make to your d-bot?'

'I kept the tail with the ball,' Charlie said. 'But I made it more like an allosaurus.'

Hunter's mind worked fast.

'Smart move,' Hunter said. 'Your allo d-bot could battle the steg and win for sure.'

Thud! Thud! Braaaaapt!

Thud! Thud! Phrrrrrrrrrr!

'Here comes our farty-bum dinosaur now!' Charlie said. 'Good thing it moves so slowly. Are you nearly done?'

Hunter looked around. 'I need a bit more time. **Quick**, grab those plants by the waterfall. It was eating them when I found it.'

Charlie ran towards the waterfall. 'Okay, I'll lead it away from you. Work fast! It might not like these as much as the moss.'

Hunter put the last panels back on his d-bot's belly. *That will have to do,* he thought. *I don't want to leave Charlie alone with that steg for too long.*

He stood the d-bot on its legs and climbed on. *You'd better work. We have no time to lose.*

Hunter hit the remote's start button. His d-bot moved forward. **'Yes!'** he cried. 'Now let's see what else still works.'

Hunter checked his d-bot over. He tried to make the wings open, but couldn't. Then he noticed how quiet it was in the clearing now.

The only sound to be heard was the waterfall.

All at once, Hunter knew what was wrong. *No* **farts**, *no* **stomps**, *no Charlie. She's taken the dinosaur too far away. I need to get going!*

'Charlie to Hunter,' came Charlie's voice from Hunter's d-band.

'I'm ready,' Hunter replied. 'The wings still don't work, but that's okay for now. I can see where you are on my d-band. I'm coming.'

'No!' Charlie snapped. 'It's not okay. Come on my d-bot. It's hidden in the ferns behind you. Hurry!'

But I've just fixed mine, thought Hunter.

Hunter knew by now, though, that Charlie was smart. *I don't get it, but I have to trust her,* he thought.

'Going to your d-bot now,' Hunter said. 'Don't worry. It's okay. Over and out.'

But when Hunter found Charlie, nothing was okay.

Chapter Four

Charlie was trapped. She'd backed into the side of a cliff. The steg had followed. It was a dead end. So Charlie had climbed the only tree there.

Hunter arrived to see the steg raising its front legs. It slammed them, one after the other, into the tree trunk.

Thud! Thud! Thud! Thud!

It's so tall standing on its back legs, he thought. *It can't move any closer to the tree trunk. Or its front legs will reach Charlie!*

Charlie was gripping the tallest branch. She couldn't go any higher.

Suddenly the steg's tail began whipping around. It swung to the right, and then to the left. Over and over, its spiky tail hit the tree trunk.

Smash! Smash! Smash! Smash!

Smash! Smash! Smash! Smash!

Charlie hung on tightly. The tree swayed. 'It can smell the moss on my hands,' she cried.

'And it thinks you have more,' added Hunter.

'But I don't,' Charlie said. 'I know it won't eat me. But it will fight me and squash me!'

'Not when there's an allo to battle with,' Hunter shouted back. 'I'm riding its favourite battle buddy, thanks to you.'

Time to play, steg, Hunter
thought, planning to win.

Hunter looked at Charlie's
remote. *What's this button?* It
had a small drawing of a
speaker on it. *Is this what I
think it is? Oh, that's really cool!*

Hunter landed the d-bot so badly that he was thrown off. *At least I didn't crash it!* he thought. He brushed himself off. *But what did Charlie mean about teleporting? And what else don't I know?*

'Charlie, why aren't you coming down?' Hunter called.

'We have to be above the dino for teleporting to work,' she said.

Hunter thought back to the dinos he'd already caught. *I must have just been lucky*. Then Charlie said, 'And when they're *really* big, it takes two rays.'

Hunter blinked.

Pppffft. Thud! Thud! Braaaaapt! Plop!

'Here it comes,' Hunter said. 'What's the plan?'

'Feed it again,' Charlie said. 'It's such a greedy dinosaur.'

Hunter nodded. 'While it's eating, I'll fly up and shoot a ray, and you can—'

'Shoot my ray from here at the same time,' Charlie finished.

'Exactly,' said Hunter, grinning.

Chapter Five

Hunter raced around gathering
up plants and ferns. In no time,
he'd built a mound of steg food
at the base of Charlie's tree.

'Get ready!' Charlie called, dropping tree branches on the growing pile. 'The steg is getting very close.

Thud! Thud! Braaaaapt!

Thud! Thud! Phrrrrrrrrrrr!

'When it gets to this pile of food, we teleport it,' Hunter said.

'Yes! Now go!' Charlie cried.

Hunter ran to Charlie's d-bot and climbed on. As the d-bot left the ground, Hunter smiled. *I needed working wings to ray the dino from above,* he thought. *Charlie's so smart!*

Flrrrrrppppppttttt! Braaaaapt!

'Aaaargh!' cried Hunter. 'Moss farts are worse – like a thick fog. I can't see where I'm going!'

'We'll have to use our ears instead,' Charlie said into the fog of gas.

Hunter hovered and listened. *Follow the farts*, he thought.

Hunter flew to the back of the steg. 'Is it eating?' he whispered into his d-band.

'Sure is,' Charlie whispered back. 'Are you above the stinky end?'

Braaaaapt! Plop!

'Yep! Ready when you are.'

Charlie counted down. 'Three, two...'

Phrrrrrrrrrrr!
Flrrrrrppppppttttt!

'One!'

Through the fog of gas, two
rays shone down on the steg.
One ray was on its front. The
other was on its back.

Charlie and Hunter listened.
Soon, the only sound they
heard was the waterfall.

'I think we did it!' Charlie cried.

'Yep!' Hunter agreed.

'I know you did,' Ms Stegg's voice boomed through their d-bands. 'Well done, D-Bot Squad team!'

Hunter had a huge grin on his face. He couldn't see Charlie's face, but he knew she would be smiling too.

'D-Bot team,' Ms Stegg said, 'you can't come back to base yet. There is another dinosaur on the loose. It's heading your way.'

'What is it?' Charlie asked.

'An argentinosaurus,' Ms Stegg replied.

Hunter and Charlie went quiet. They were thinking.

'Our d-bots are made to catch stegs,' Charlie whispered. 'How are we going to do this?'

'You need to change your d-bots quickly,' said Ms Stegg. 'Together, you can do this. Oh no, another screen is flashing. I have to go. **Think big!** Over and out.'

'**Wait!**' Charlie cried, breathing fast. 'This dino is heavier and longer than ten stegs!'

But Ms Stegg was gone.

'Charlie,' Hunter said firmly, 'this gas is lifting. And I have an idea. But first we need to get back to my d-bot.'

Chapter Six

Back at the waterfall, Charlie and Hunter were busy. Their heads were close together. They were talking and working on their d-bots.

'Your idea of joining our d-bots together is clever, Hunter,' Charlie said.

'We need to be as big as we can,' Hunter replied. 'But we need to know how we can win, too. We need good add-ons. What are you thinking?'

While Charlie shared her ideas with Hunter, the argentino was getting closer. And closer.

Unaware, the pair worked on quietly together. *I should be freaking out about this dinosaur,* thought Hunter. *But it's good building dino-bots with Charlie.*

Charlie passed Hunter some extend-o-rods from her tool belt. 'For our d-bot's neck,' she said, smiling. Then she went straight back to work.

'Thanks,' said Hunter. 'Our d-bot's neck will be better than a real argentino neck.'

'It needs to be,' Charlie replied.

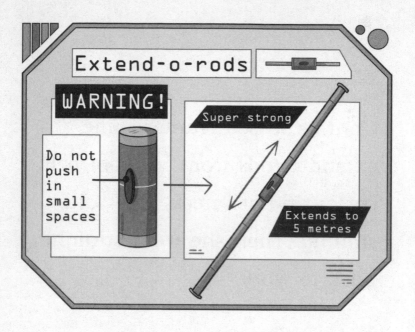

Extend-o-rods

WARNING!

Do not push in small spaces

Super strong

Extends to 5 metres

'I think our new double d-bot is just about done,' said Hunter. 'What do you think?'

Charlie opened a panel on the double d-bot's belly. 'Let's fill this space with plants and ferns.'

'Good thinking!' said Hunter.

And then they heard...

'Roooaar! Raaaah!' Sniifffff! Snoooort!

'The argentino,' Charlie cried.
'It can smell the waterfall!'

Hunter and Charlie climbed
onto their double d-bot. Then
they clipped their remotes to
their belts.

Hunter could hear Charlie
breathing fast again.

'We can do this, Charlie,' Hunter said. 'We're a great team.'

Just then, the argentino swung its head over the treetops.

Hunter and Charlie gasped at what they saw.

Another D-bot Squad member was swinging from the argentino's head.

Big Stink

First published by Allen & Unwin in 2017

Allen & Unwin
83 Alexander Street
Crows Nest NSW 2065
Australia
Phone: (61 2) 8425 0100
Email: info@allenandunwin.com
Web: www.allenandunwin.com

A Cataloguing-in-Publication entry is
available from the National Library of Australia
www.trove.nla.gov.au

ISBN 978 1 76029 600 1

For teaching resources, explore
www.allenandunwin.com/resources/for-teachers

Cover and text design by Sandra Nobes
Set in 16 pt ITC Stone Informal by Sandra Nobes
This book was printed in April 2017 at
McPherson's Printing Group, Australia.

1 3 5 7 9 10 8 6 4 2

macparkbooks.com

MIX
Paper from
responsible sources
FSC® C001695

The paper in this book is FSC® certified.
FSC® promotes environmentally responsible,
socially beneficial and economically viable
management of the world's forests.

What will Hunter
and Charlie do?
Read Book 5, *Stack Attack,*
to find out...